25

W9-BEY-446

JJ
PARENT-TEACHER
Tym

Published in the United States by
QEB Publishing, Inc.
23062 La Cadena Drive
Laguna Hills, CA 92653

www.qeb-publishing.com

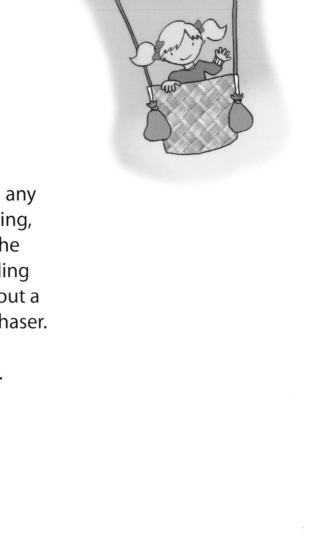

Library of Congress Control Number has been applied for.

ISBN 978 1 59566 591 1

Author Kate Tym
Illustrator Sarah Wade
Editor Clare Weaver
Designer Alix Wood
Consultant David Hart

Publisher Steve Evans
Creative Director Zeta Davies

Printed and bound in the United States

QEB

MANNERS

Time to SHARE

KATE TYM

Illustrated by
Sarah Wade

Sarah and Clara were twins. Their mom and dad liked to give them **lots** and **lots** of nice toys.

So, from the moment they were born, Sarah and Clara Brown were very lucky indeed.

There were two four-poster cots, two turbo-drive, fuel-injected, remote-controlled, leather-lined strollers and two solid-gold potties.

NEW IN!
Super-deluxe
four-poster cot

5

If Daddy gave something to one baby, the other one screamed until she had just the same.

"Don't you worry," clucked Mommy, handing out yet more toys. "There are plenty of toys for you both to play with."

As they got older,
Sarah and Clara
wanted more and more.

8

The twins knew exactly how to get what they wanted. Mr. and Mrs. Brown gave in to them every time.

"Sarah wants a palace playhouse with five towers, turrets, and a moat," Mrs. Brown said, reaching for her laptop.

"Clara wants a skyscraper playhouse with a glass lift," said Mr. Brown, searching for the phone number of his architect.

So, Sarah lived in her perfect palace with a fabulous zoo and adventure playground in the garden.

And Clara lived in her skyscraper and could ride the lift down to her funfair, filled with magical rides and flashing lights.

It was everything she'd ever dreamed of. Except for one thing... She had no one to share it with.

13

Sarah was starting to feel lonely, too. She walked over to her adventure playground, climbed the ladder to the enormous slide, and slid down it.

"**Wheee!**" she screamed,

but inside she felt sad.

She decided to go around
to Clara's and invite her
to come and play.

At the same time, Clara had the same idea.

Sarah and Clara met in the middle, in front of their parents' mansion and gave each other a great big hug!

They took turns feeding the animals and whizzing down the "Flying Fox."

After you.

No, after you.

19

And at the end of the day, they sat down exhausted and happy—together.

And... that's exactly what they did!

WHEEEEEE!

Notes for parents and teachers

- Look at the front cover of the book together. Talk about the picture. Can the children guess what the book is going to be about? Read the title together.

- Sarah and Clara's parents had a lot of money to buy things for their children (pages 4–5). Discuss with the children whether Sarah and Clara needed everything their parents bought them. Do the children understand the difference between needing something and wanting something?

- Read pages 8–9 together. Do the girls ask nicely for the things they want? Do the children think that the girls expect to receive everything they want? Discuss whether sometimes having less might make you care more about the things you have. Talk about this in the context of toys the children have. Do they have some things they don't take particular care of or some things they really value? What does it mean to value something?

- What do the children think would happen if Mr. and Mrs. Brown said "no" to their daughters' requests?

- Ask the children to imagine what it would be like to live in a fabulous palace or skyscraper. How much fun would it really be to live there on their own? Would they feel lonely? Would they feel a bit scared?

- Read pages 14–15. Ask the children why they think Sarah is feeling sad inside. Does having lots of things make them happy? What does make them happy?

- Get the children to compare pages 12–15 with pages 18–19. If living in a palace with a zoo and a funfair wouldn't be much fun on their own, how might it be with a good friend to share it with? Talk about taking turns. Is it easier to do things one at a time sometimes? Can it be just as much fun watching someone else enjoy themselves when it's their turn? How does it make the children feel to see someone else enjoying the same things as them?

- Young children generally find it hard to share their things. Look at the last picture and discuss it with the children (pages 22–23). Could the twins go on everything at once? Does it matter that other people are using their things? Talk about ownership and the concept of borrowing things. Talk about times the children have been to someone else's house and played with their toys. Have they taken the toys home or left them when it's time to go home? Do the children think it made the twins feel happy to see their friends getting so much pleasure out of all their things? Why might that be?